For Poppy — J.D.

A TEMPLAR BOOK

First published in the UK in 2018 by Templar Publishing,
an imprint of Kings Road Publishing,
part of the Bonnier Publishing Group,
The Plaza, 535 King's Road, London, SW10 0SZ
www.templarco.co.uk
www.bonnierpublishing.com

1  3  5  7  9  10  8  6  4  2

ISBN: 978-1-78741-109-8

Designed by Genevieve Webster
Edited by Joanna McInerney

Printed in China

# LONG DOG

By James Davies

templar
books

This is me.

This is my dog.

Have you noticed anything special about him?

Yep.

He's LONG!

That's why we call him Long Dog.

I don't know why he's so long.
Maybe it's his dog food.

Maybe his Mum and Dad were made of spaghetti.

Maybe he's secretly a snake.

He wasn't a very long puppy.

But he soon grew longer . . .

and LONGER . . . and LONGER!

Mum and Dad think he's becoming a bit of a problem.

He's MINE and he's the BEST
and we do EVERYTHING together.

Sometimes we go to the moon.

Sometimes we do yoga.

Sometimes we do building.

And sometimes we eat broccoli.

ANYTHING is possible when you're with Long Dog.

When we go to the park, the other dogs don't look like Long Dog.

There are skinny ones,

ROUND ones,

BIG ones

and mini ones!

But I've NEVER seen a long dog like Long Dog.

My friends even started to say mean things about him.

So we went to play on our own.

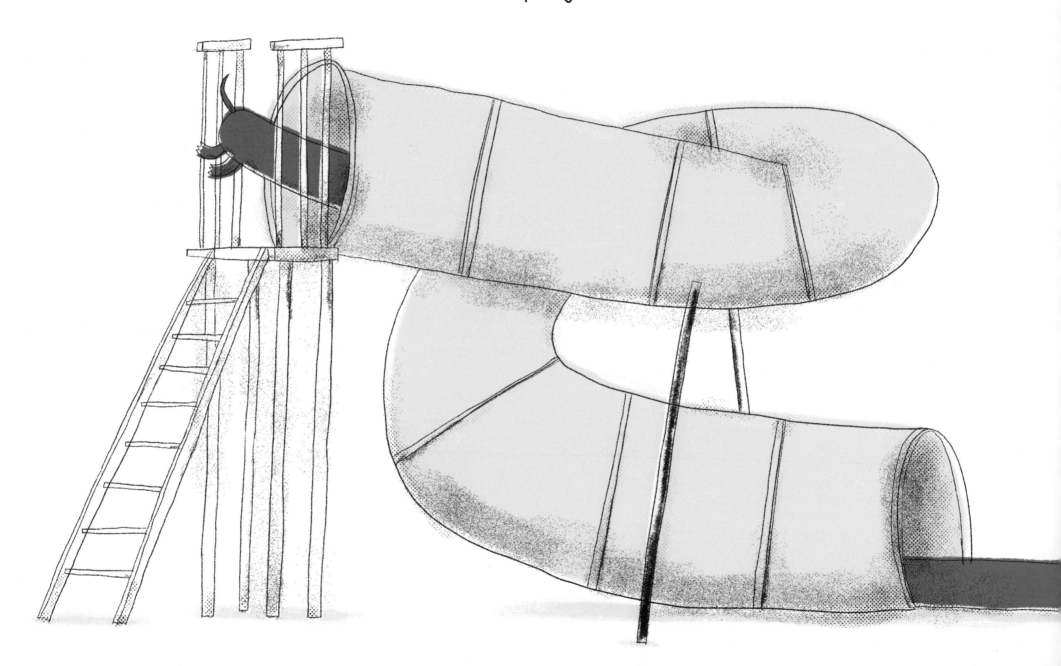

But suddenly we heard . . .

"Our dogs have

I looked at Long Dog.
Long Dog looked at me.

I knew EXACTLY what he was thinking.
He wanted me to follow him!

We searched everywhere for the other dogs.
And by everywhere, I mean nearly the WHOLE sandpit.

They were nowhere to be seen.

But just then,
Long Dog found a clue . . .

"FOLLOW THAT

He led us to a hole.

# THE MOST GIGANTO-NORMOUS HOLE EVER!

Where had it come from?

We looked inside
and it soon became obvious.
Darling Bella had been
digging again!
And right at the bottom were . . .

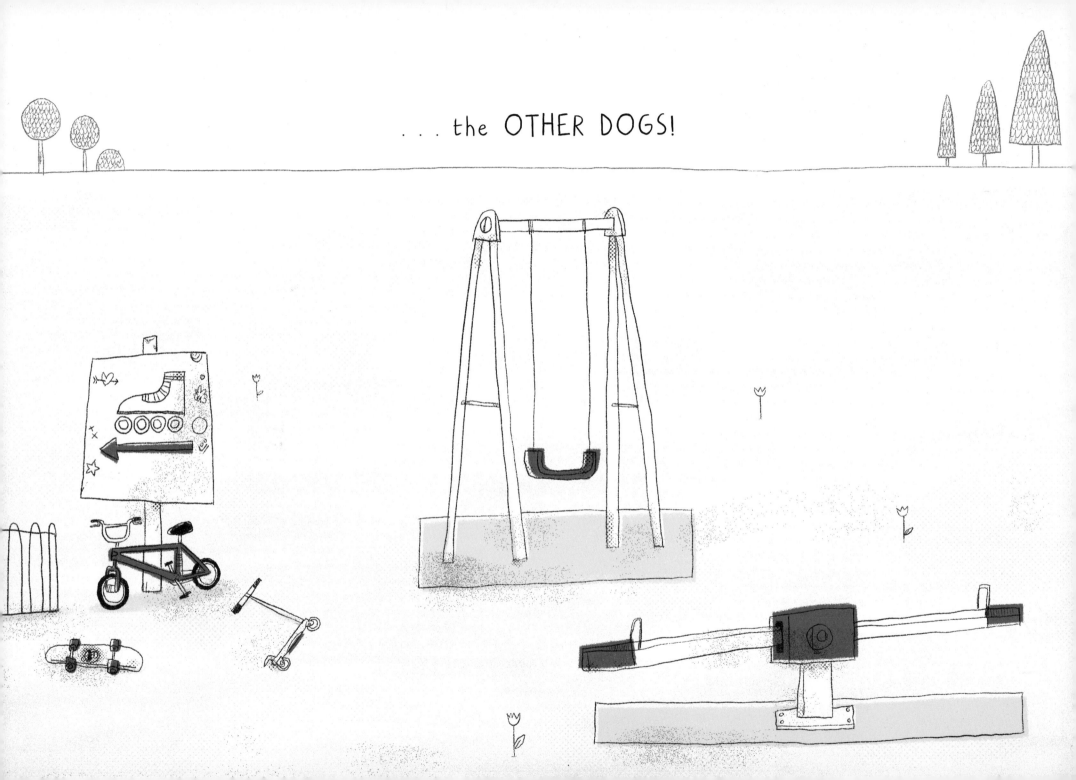

. . . the OTHER DOGS!

How would we ever get them out?
We'd need something long . . . something REALLY long.

Before I could come up with a plan,
Long Dog went straight down the hole!

One by one, he rescued all the dogs. Even REALLY BIG Arnold!

My good boy Long Dog had saved the day!

After that, even Mum and Dad changed their minds about him.

And now, no one thinks Long Dog is weird any more. In fact . . . .

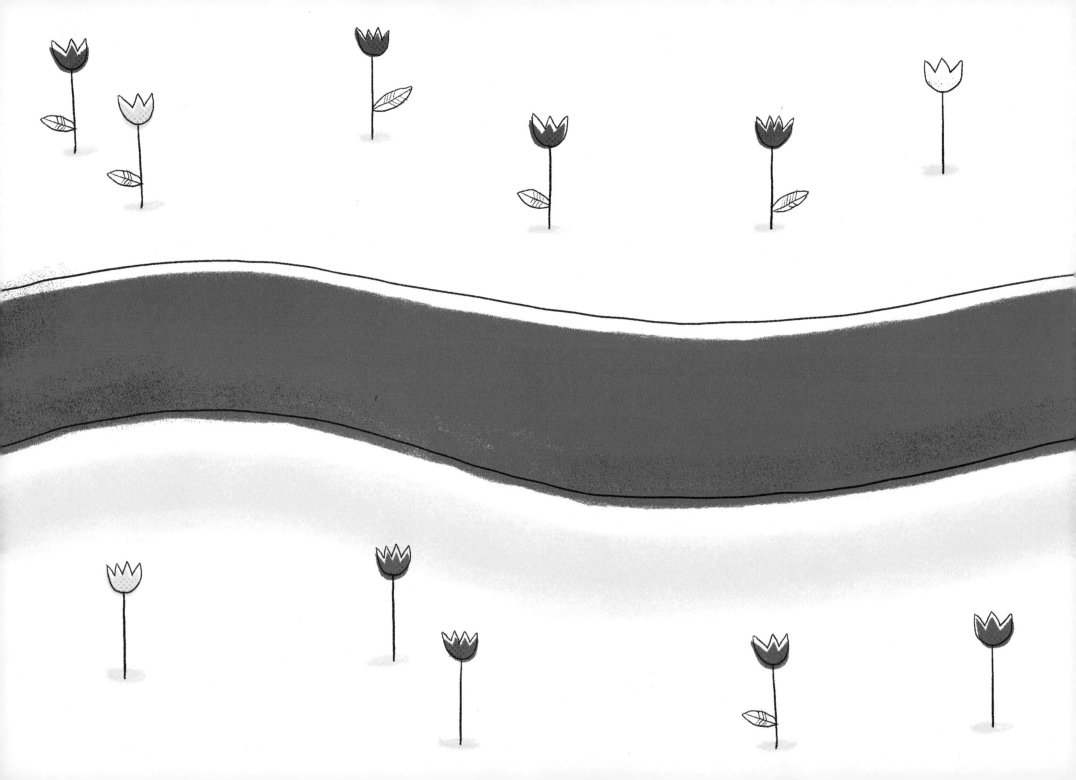